The Littles
Do Their Homework

Adapted from *The Littles Go To School* and
The Littles Give a Party by John Peterson.
The Littles Go To School Copyright © 1983 by John Peterson.
The Littles Give a Party Copyright © 1972 by John Peterson.

ISBN 0-439-42497-6

12 11 10 9 8 7 6 5 4 3 2 1   2 3 4 5 6 7/0

Printed in the U.S.A.
First Scholastic printing, October 2002

The Littles Do Their Homework

Adapted by **Teddy Slater**
from *THE LITTLES GO TO SCHOOL*
and *THE LITTLES GIVE A PARTY*
by **John Peterson**
Illustrated by **Jacqueline Rogers**

SCHOLASTIC INC.
New York   Toronto   London   Auckland   Sydney
Mexico City   New Delhi   Hong Kong   Buenos Aires

Tom and Lucy Little

were good students.

They knew how to read.

They knew how to write.

They could add and subtract

very well.

But Tom and Lucy

didn't go to school.

School came to them!

Their teacher was Ms. Beta Gogg.

She came once a month

to give them their lessons.

Cousin Dinky Little brought her

in his glider.

Cousin Dinky landed on the roof
of the Bigg family's house.
That's where the Little family lived,
right inside the walls.

There were seven Littles
in the house.
They were so tiny
and so quiet,
the Biggs never knew they
lived there!

Ms. Gogg stayed
for two days each month.
But she gave Tom and Lucy
enough homework to last
until her next visit.

This month, Tom and Lucy

had to write a science report

about animals.

They began with

the Biggs's cat, Hildy.

They already knew a lot
about Hildy.
Tom had made friends
with her long ago.

Tom and Lucy also knew

the Biggs's gerbils.

Littles and gerbils

are a lot alike.

They're both very small.

They both have nice

long tails.

And they both like to play.

"The Biggs have some chickens

out back," Tom said.

"Let's write about them, too."

"But chickens are too wild,"

said Lucy.

"Mom and Dad don't even want us

to go *near* the henhouse."

"I bet Ms. Gogg would give
us an A-plus if we put those
chickens in our report," Tom said.
"We could even get a real
egg to show her!"
"But how?" Lucy asked.
Tom told Lucy his plan.

Very early the next morning,

Lucy and Tom met in front of

the tin-can elevator.

The elevator went down

to a secret door

on the first floor.

A few minutes later,

Tom and Lucy were outside!

It was still dark.

The henhouse was
way across the backyard.
It took the Littles a
long time to get there.

"P.U.!" Lucy said.

"I never knew chickens

smelled so bad."

"Let's grab an egg

and get out of here," Tom said.

Uh-oh!

The egg was heavy.

Lucy and Tom had to roll the

egg across the floor.

It was hard work.

Soon, the two Littles

were huffing and puffing.

Suddenly, one of the chickens woke up.

"CLUCK! CLUCK!" she said.

Another chicken woke up.

And then another.

The chickens all flew down

to the floor.

"CLUCK! CLUCK! CLUCK!"
The chickens screeched
and squawked.

"I think it's time to go,"

Lucy said.

"Good thinking," Tom said.

But it was too late.

The chickens were

blocking the way out.

"CLUCK! CLUCK! CLUCK!"

The chickens came closer.

"Hide, Lucy!" Tom yelled.

The two Littles jumped

into a pile of straw.

Just then, the front door of the

henhouse flew open.

It was Mr. Bigg!

"What's all the noise

about?" he said.

Of course, no one answered.

Tom and Lucy

ran outside as fast as they could.

They were back in bed

before the sun came up.

Tom and Lucy never got
an egg. But the next time Ms. Gogg
came, they had a fine
science report — and a very
wild tale to tell.